It will not be easy and I advise you to be very careful. Doctor Watson and I have often found ourselves in grave peril while solving our famous cases. The truth seldom comes easily when called, especially when some of the world's most calculating villains are determined that it should remain hidden.

I have faith in you, and in myself, that together we will be able to bring the truth to light and ease the suffering of the poor souls who have come to me for help.

So, what do you say, dear reader, will you be my Watson? The answer is surely elementary.

Yours faithfully,

Sherlock Holmes

The Cherry in the Cake

30th March 1893

Perhaps the most unsavoury of mysteries was served with a pot of strong tea at Baker Street this afternoon. A priceless ruby of unknown origin lodged into an exceptionally well-baked cherry cake that had been left on my doorstep. Mrs Hudson had to rescue it before the pigeons noticed.

On opening up the package, it became clear that we weren't the first to enjoy the moist appearance of this delicious cake. Someone had cut themselves a large slice and appeared to have taken a bite, because there, lodged in the slice, quite plainly, was the largest ruby I had ever laid eyes on.

But how did this jewel find its way into a cherry cake? It reminds me of 'The Adventure of the Blue Carbuncle' in which the Countess of Morcar's diamond was discovered inside a Christmas goose.

There were some interesting notes upon the paper in which it was wrapped.

114 Regents Walk
29th March. 2.30 pm.

· THE ·
CASEBOOKS OF
SHERLOCK
HOLMES

Featuring four mysteries to solve:

The Cherry in the Cake

The Adventure of the Cursed Cartouche

The Terror of Traymar House

The Adventure of the Vanishing Lord

Dear Reader,

I am writing to you in the highly unfamiliar position of requiring assistance. My usually trusty companion, Doctor Watson, has been called away on a most inconvenient family emergency and I have been left to tend to my cases alone.

As my fame as a detective has grown, people from across the globe have come to my home in Baker Street for help with all manner of mysteries. I have solved kidnappings and blackmail, and I've even located the odd missing pet. Without Doctor Watson at my side, there are simply too many cases for me to solve alone.

In this book, you will find four new and exciting adventures that I have thus far been unable to untangle. I have gathered together all of the evidence: statements from witnesses, newspaper articles, diaries, receipts and photographs of the scenes of the crime, organising them alongside my notes. Your mission is to decode the clues on the pages to solve each of the crimes.

This note was also tucked into the package:

GF – for your consideration and enjoyment. I hope this changes your mind.

Mrs Hudson had some thoughts when I questioned how such a jewel could be missing without anyone noticing.

"Oh, Mr Holmes, you've been so busy. Have you not heard that London has been abuzz with the news of Lady Swinbrook's stolen ruby? Perhaps you missed it, because the culprit has already been arrested. The jewel was not recovered. Quite the mystery."

You will see, dear reader, how keenly I am in need of your help.

Yours,

SH

LONDON CHRONICLE

ILLUSTRATED WEEKLY NEWSPAPER
ISSUE NO .947

CURTAINS FOR LOCAL DRAPER

Shock at the arrest of Miss Mimi Swathe after the theft of a valuable ruby from Swinbrook Hall, South Kensington.

Lady Swinbrook alerted the local police to the loss of the stone from her chamber at 1 p.m., shortly after Miss Mimi Swathe had visited the hall to measure up for new curtains for the east wing of the hall.

Miss Mimi Swathe was arrested at 2.30 p.m. as she returned to her shop.

The stone, the famous red-throat ruby, is still missing.

Clients of Miss Swathe are instructed to contact her colleague, Miss Swag, at their shop – Swathe's and Swag's.

Before heading to the hall, take a look at what Detective Swan observed when he answered Lady Swinbrook's call:

DETECTIVE SWAN -
POLICE NOTES

Arrived at Swinbrook Hall 1.15 p.m.

Met by housekeeper - Miss Boyle
- shown in to Lady Swinbrook's
chamber. Interesting chalk marks
on the dresser.

Showed myself out at 2.45 p.m.
as Miss Boyle had to step out.

Lady Swinbrook very distressed.

WITNESS STATEMENT   Miss Boyle

The room was in good order when I showed
Miss Swathe in. I had to leave to attend to
something in the kitchen. She left before
I was done. The next time I came into this
room was when Lady Swinbrook rang the
bell. As soon as she told me her ruby was
missing I ran straight downstairs and sent
the kitchen maid out to fetch the police. I
was surprised by how quickly you arrived.
If that is all, I must get back to the
kitchen. There is a lot of baking to do for
Lady Swinbrook's luncheon this weekend.

Swathe's & Swag's
78 HIGH STREET

CLOSING DOWN SALE!

Final day 12 April
Everything must go!

Going out of business? Were times hard at Swathe's and Swag's?

Is M desperate for money?

Sorry M. GF says loan is a no go.

Need to find funds elsewhere.

All my love. MT. x

WITNESS STATEMENT   Miss Mimi Swathe

Arrested: 3.30 p.m.

I arrived at 11 a.m. and met with Lady Swinbrook
in the parlour. She chose some fabrics and then
the housekeeper showed me up to her lady's
chamber. The first I had heard of any ruby
was when you mentioned it just now. All I took
were pictures and measurements. Miss Boyle, the
housekeeper, showed me out at 12.30 p.m. I left
and went straight to the fabric wholesaler
to buy the material for the curtains.

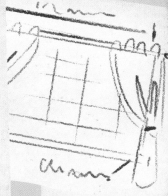

Miss Swathe was arrested as she was returning to her shop. She was carrying bolts of fabric. No ruby was found about her person. Could she have stashed it somewhere?

The cake came wrapped in paper with an appointment written on it. Time to see who has an appointment at 114 Regents Walk and what it is for.

114 Regents Walk
29th March, 2.30 p.m.

CLARENCE YANKIT
GENERAL DENTIST

CLARENCE YANKIT

Dentistry and oral care

If your teeth say "ow!"
he'll take care of them now.

114 Regents Walk

Thursday - to remember:

Order more hog bristle toothbrushes

Clean extraction pliers

GF — broken tooth
Send bill to 58 High Street

Visit Hartnett's to collect natural tooth replacements taken from the mouths of dead soldiers

GF — is there something familiar about those initials?

A small stack of cards were placed on the reception desk under a little sign saying:

'Struggling to pay your bill? Maybe we can help.'

Gideon Frump

Savings and Loans

Ask and ye shall receive
(within reason)

58 High Street

While leafing through a magazine on the counter, a sweet article brought back fond memories of the delicious cherry cake:

Kensington Life MAGAZINE

Your local news brought to you   ISSUE 79

MYSTERY BAKER WINS AGAIN

The Swinbrook Fete's cake contest was won for the 7th year in a row by the mysterious Moira Bea Lenny. She was awarded her 7th rainbow ribbon, but once again was unable to collect her prize.

There was an excellent turn-out this year in all categories. A very special mention goes to Mr Berry for his savoury cake creation, which did not place.

Mrs M. Hubert finally took first prize in the tarts category with her delicate strawberry tartlets.

SWEET TOOTH?

Come and support Moira Bea Lenny's planning application for a new tea shop and bakery on 12th April.

Time to speak to Gideon Frump. It seems with this cake he has bitten off rather more than he could chew.

WITNESS STATEMENT   Gideon Frump

Oh dear! I had hoped you wouldn't find me. I left the ruby with you because I felt certain you would ensure its return to its owner. I didn't want the scandal. Theft and banks don't go well together. Stolen goods showing up… I'd be ruined!

What kind of person puts a ruby in a cherry cake? It was delicious, well what I had, but I broke my tooth as I bit down on the hidden gem. I got my assistant to make an appointment at the dentist, which he did after putting something in the safe.

The cake was left on my desk. People do funny things when they are in need of money.

One mystery is solved. But how did the ruby get into the cake and why would whoever put it there leave the cake for Mr Frump? Was Mimi Swathe in need of a loan?

What did his assistant put in the safe? I asked Mr Frump if we could take a look.

WITNESS STATEMENT   Gideon Frump

Another cake! My assistant must have put it in the safe. Martin isn't here today, otherwise you could ask him.

Alongside the cake, I discovered this note and a mouthwatering recipe:

Prize-winning recipe! Please put in the safe.
– MB

A long bake. Could the suspect have made it to the fabric wholesaler, baked a cake and got it to the bank before she was arrested?

Cherry Cake

Ingredients

1 lb. flour
6 oz. butter
6 oz. sugar
3 eggs
4 drops vanilla essence
6 oz. cherries

Method

Mix all ingredients together and bake for 1 ½ hours.

23

Let us take a look at the desk of the assistant, Martin Tudor.

I know he's turned us down, but how about if he tastes it? Give him this. Put the other in the safe. The ingredients of this cake are very special, indeed. I hope we don't need it, but it's there if we do.

If we get what we want on the 12th, we'll need money fast.

All my love. MB

Can Mimi Swathe be both an award-winning baker and an excellent seamstress? I headed to her business to see if there was anything that had been missed by Detective Swan. She is the prime suspect, but should she be?

WITNESS STATEMENT — Miss Leonora Swag

Search by all means. Mimi is innocent. We didn't need the money. We're closing the shop to concentrate on making curtains for the great houses in the neighbourhood. Our order book is full to bursting! The sooner she's found innocent, the sooner she can get back to work. We thought we had a buyer for the shop - a tea room or something - but we haven't heard from them in a while.

FLITWICK'S FINE FABRICS
32 WINDEN AVENUE

ITEM	PRICE
20 yd Violet Damask Silk	12s 6d per yd.

Always a pleasure to do business with you, Ms Swathe. I hope to see even more of you after the 12th. Best of luck!

F. Flitwick

RLG BANK

58 High Street, London

LOAN APPLICATION

Applicants:	Ms Swathe & Ms Swag
Loan amount:	£200
Loan purpose:	Business venture
Loan assessed by:	G. Frump

4 PIECES   **BLUE**

BASSET'S BLUE
tailor's chalk

Keep your patterns true –
Choose chalk that's blue!

RLG BANK

58 High Street, London

BUSINESS LOAN

Swathe's and Swag's – curtains and upholstery

LOAN APPROVED

Can you spot any differences between this and Detective Swan's picture at Swinbrook?

This was pasted up on a board by the door. Is anything else happening on 12th April?

PLANNING APPLICATION MEETING

12th April

To discuss possibility of conversion of

Swathe's and Swag's Drapers

to

tea room

Swathe's & Swag's

78 HIGH STREET

CLOSING DOWN SALE!

RIBBON sold out in all colours

Final day 12th April
Everything must go!

There was also this notice.
The closing-down sale is going well!

I felt another visit to Swinbrook Hall was in order. As Miss Boyle was out, I took the opportunity to ask the maid to show me to her office.

There were certainly some interesting discoveries.

Menu for luncheon

Light soup. Salad. Fish. Vegetables.

– Let's keep it light. No baked goods.

Typical

A rainbow of ribbons.
Is there one missing?

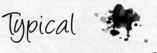 Collins
Construction Ltd

Building estimate

Conversion of property,
Swathe's and Swag's - £50

£25 deposit required
ASAP for go-ahead

Also in Miss Boyle's room was a copy of Moira Bea Lenny's book. I tore out the introduction.

Marianne Boyle

The Housekeeper's Handbook
By Moira Bea Lenny

Dedicated to my fiancé, MT.

Welcome to my book! Inside, you will discover everything you need to know regarding house management.

As a housekeeper at one of the finest homes in London, I've seen everything, and will be able to guide you through the ups and downs of life both above and below stairs.

My mistress, like so many fashionable ladies, is a fan of a light diet and does not enjoy baked goods, so when not tending to her fine home or preparing her meals, I can be found at the stove baking. I am an award-winning baker and enjoy baking cakes for competitions. I hope one day to open my own tea room.

My darling Marianne.

How I long to call you my wife.

One day we will live and work side by side.

Your ever-devoted MT xx

MT? Could this be the MT we have met before? Has there been a mix-up with his fiancée?

An interesting mix of evidence. Here are a few questions to help discern the ingredients in this delicious deception:

1. What colour is the tailor's chalk on Lady Swinbrook's dresser?

2. Is there anything in the magazine article that might 'tie' someone to the crime?

3. Were any ingredients left at the scene of the crime?

4. Why might you be out of luck if you wanted to buy ribbons?

5. Do two names share the same sweet ambitions?

Time to reflect on the evidence.

Discover the fate of the ruby by holding the opposite page against a mirror.

Well done, reader! As divine as the results proved to be (it really was a most excellent cherry cake), you correctly digested the clues and discovered the plan was half-baked.

Miss Boyle, having received notice that her loan application had been rejected, was desperate for money to start her own tea shop. When Miss Swathe came to measure for curtains in Lady Swinbrook's chamber, Miss Boyle saw her chance to have the perfect alibi for taking the ruby.

After showing Miss Swathe out, she hastily rushed back upstairs to grab the ruby, leaving a mess of flour and her winning purple ribbon in her wake. She only planned to use it if Gideon Frump turned her loan application down again after tasting her delicious cake. When the police were alerted so quickly, Miss Boyle panicked and hid the ruby in the cakes she was baking to convince Gideon Frump to loan her the money, after all. She smuggled the cakes out to her fiancé at the bank. Unfortunately for Miss Boyle, in her haste, she labelled the cakes wrongly.

Had she not done so, Gideon Frump may never have taken that fateful bite that sent him to Clarence Yankit and led you to her fiancé, Martin Tudor, in which case Miss Mimi Swathe may have been punished for a crime of which she was not guilty.

And what of Moira Bea Lenny? Who is she and does she plan to open a rival tea shop? No. Moira Bea Lenny and Marianne Boyle are one and the same housekeeper, fiancée, author, award-winning baker and thief.

The Adventure of the Cursed Cartouche

An English nobleman and his beloved dog found dead within days of one another. Were they struck down by the ancient curse of an unfortunate pharaoh or slain by someone close at hand?

Monthaven Manor, Somerset
August, 1886

Dear Mr Holmes,

I am writing because I do not know where else to turn. You may have read about the sudden death of my employer, the 6th Earl of Somerset. I found him myself, lying in his study, a find from a recent excavation clasped in one hand and a letter from the Egyptian Minister of Antiquities in the other.

The staff are heartbroken at the loss of our dear earl who, though a stickler for cleanliness, was a fair master. The earl's death was pronounced unexplained by Dr Manwell, the family physician, and then, yesterday, the earl's dog, Anubis, was also found dead in the earl's study. Coincidence? I think not, for the cartouche the earl had been sent the day of his death has gone missing.

I have enclosed a sketch the earl must have made shortly before he died. I can only think both the earl and his dog are victims of some dreadful curse on the tomb he and his partner, Harold Caper, have been in search of all these years. Now the staff are living in fear that one of them will be the curse's next victim.

Please, Mr Holmes, relieve our suffering and find out the cause of these untimely deaths so that we may ~~rest in peace~~ sleep soundly in our beds once more.

Yours sincerely,

Ernest Biggins – Butler

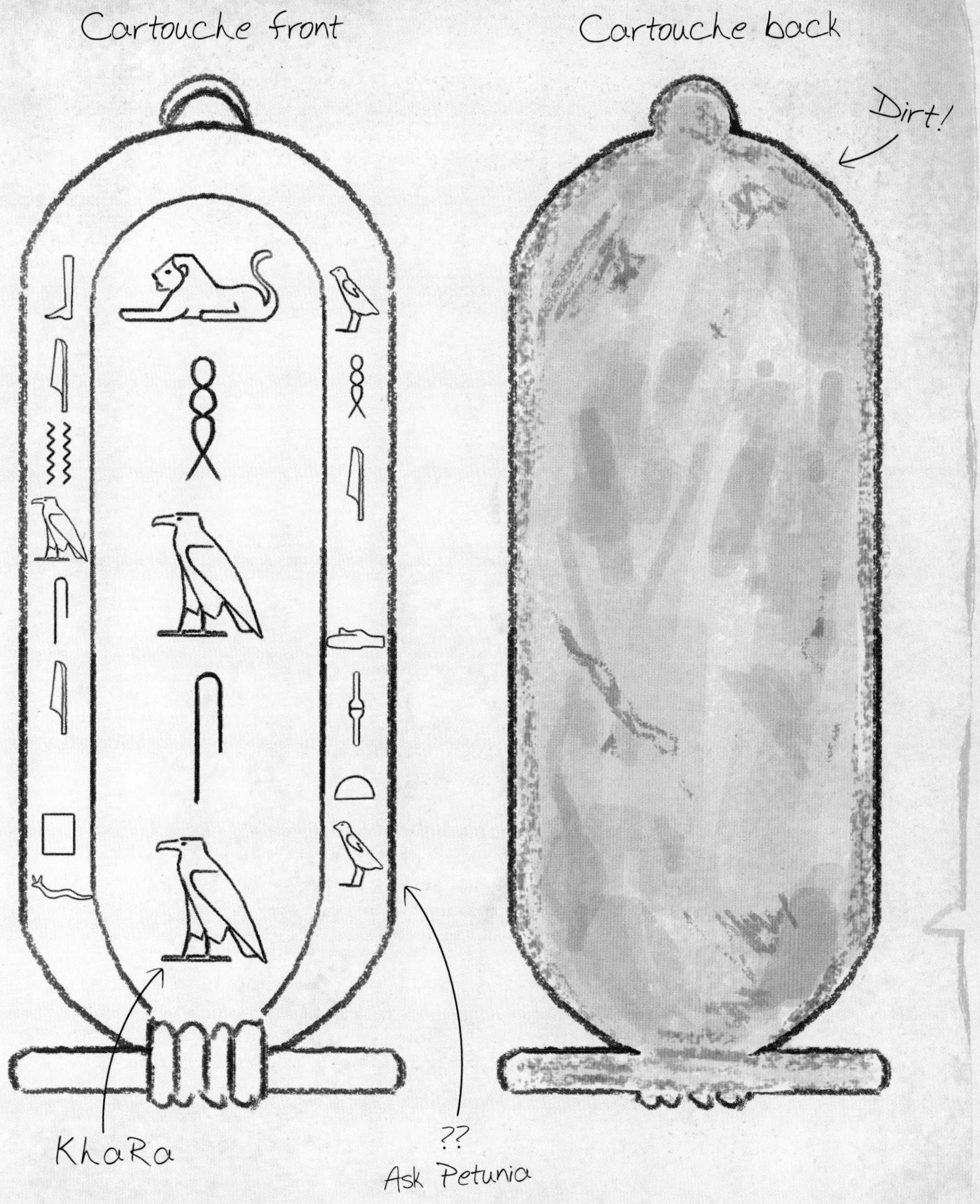

Cartouche front

Cartouche back

Dirt!

KhaRa

??
Ask Petunia

Before heading to Monthaven, a quick look at the newspapers might help us to learn a bit more about this earl and the 'curse'.

THE MODERN ARCHAEOLOGIST

DIGGING UP FRESH DIRT ON OLD STORIES

Digging up disappointment!

Written by Archibald Pollard

After a fourth year of no finds for the 6th Earl of Monthaven, will he continue or will he finally accept what many had warned him: the desert is indeed deserted?

The unfortunate pharaoh is proving to be the unfound pharaoh for the earl, who so far has only found sand, sand and yet more sand.

"If this continues, the earl may have to grab a shovel and get his own hands dirty for once. Heaven forbid!" stated Harold Caper, lead excavator and author of *Toxic Trust – Priests and Their Poisons in the Ancient World*.

Toom Doom!

Written by Walter Waters

New Egyptian Head of Department of Archaeology, Jacques Pinchart, warns of a modern curse on collectors of ancient artefacts.

"Rich men beware! The treasures of Egypt belong to Egypt alone. Take no more and return all that is not yours or prepare to meet your doom."

OBITUARIES

Quentin Frussup
6th Earl of Monthaven

Amateur Egyptologist, collector and sponsor of Harold Caper's four failed excavations in the Valley of the Kings in search of the Unfortunate Pharaoh.

The earl leaves behind devoted wife, Petunia (née Pearson), American heiress to the Pearson Railroad fortune, and children, Matilda 8 and Fergus 6.

"My darling Quentin." said Petunia Frussup. "I will continue the search for the Unfortunate Pharaoh in my husband's loving memory."

Why was the pharaoh unfortunate?

Quentin Frussup and team survey the Val...

CURSE OF THE UNFORTUNATE PHARAOH STRIKES AGAIN...

Anubis, prized pet pug belonging to the late 6th Earl of Monthaven, found dead just days after his master. Could he be the second victim of a curse placed on the tomb on the infamously Unfortunate Pharaoh, KhaRa?

"A tragedy," remarked Harold Caper, the earl's partner in excavations. "A superstitious man might suggest the curse is lashing out because we are inches away from discovery. Such a powerful curse must be protecting unimaginable treasures. I will not let this curse, or anything else, stand in the way of my search."

<u>May, 1875</u>

The 6th Earl of Monthaven, Quentin Frussup, is not the first to find fortune in the New World but has perhaps happened on the most beautiful source:

Petunia Pearson, heir to Conrad Pearson's immense railroad wealth. The happy couple intend to honeymoon where they met – among the ruins of ancient Egypt.

Petunia Pearson

Mrs Hudson did her own digging and pulled this out of the society pages for me.

The HAT SHOP

A Pug's Life

Vets warn dog owners of the danger chocolate poses to their prized pooches. Far from a sweet treat, as little as a few ounces can be fatal to our furry friends. Keep out of reach.

I took a trip to Monthaven. Take a look at what I was able to gather from the earl's study.

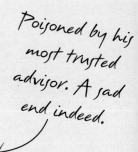

buried in a spectacularly decorated tomb in the Great Pyramids of Giza.

Archeologists have so far been unable to excavate the sarcophagus.

KhaRa
(The Unfortunate Pharaoh)
Ruler of Egypt
2455-2452 BC

Son of KhaTen, KhaRa was Murdered by his people, who believed his death would appease the gods and end a famine that plagued Egypt during his reign.

According to legend, the pharaoh was killed when he inhaled a toxic dust placed on the armrests of his throne by his most trusted vizier.

It is believed KhaRa was buried in an unmarked tomb filled with priceless treasures to further appease the gods.

KhaRa's tomb was said to be protected by a powerful curse:

'He who breathes the name KhaRa will inhale certain death.'

Poisoned by his most trusted advisor. A sad end indeed.

Harold Caper — a determined fellow with many strings to his bow.

Harold Caper
Curriculum Vitae

Graduated in ancient history and toxicology from Oxford University, 1875.

Keen amateur artist and engraver.

Head of Excavations in Valley of the Kings, Egypt. 1882 - present.

Personal statement
I have many skills and will use all of them to achieve my aims.

LONDON MUSEUM OF EGYPTOLOGY
1 KINGS ROAD AVENUE, LONDON W1

Dear Quentin,

I was pleased to meet you at the embassy.

I hear you have quite the collection of artefacts. I would like to meet with you to see them for myself and arrange for their swift return to Egypt.

Failure to do so will have the direst of consequences.

J. Pinchart

J. Pinchart
Egyptian Head of Departme

POSTAL TELEGRAPH DELIVERY CORP
TELEGRAM

POSTAL TELEGRAPH CORP TRANSMITS AND DELIVERS MESSAGES ACCORDING TO TERMS AND CONDITIONS - SEE REVERSE OF CARD

Q - SORRY YOU ARE WITHDRAWING FUNDS. AM SURE THE VALLEY STILL CONTAINS SECRETS - SENT YOU NEW FIND - APOLOGIES FOR DUST.

LONDON MUSEUM OF EGYPTOLOGY
1 KINGS ROAD AVENUE, LONDON W1

CHOC TUT'S
EGYPT'S FINEST MILK CHOCOLATE PHARAOHS
8 oz

Dear Quentin,

Farewell to your museum!

I am glad you have accepted the museum's offer for compensation. Though these treasures should never have been taken, I am pleased at their return.

Please accept this box of a half-dozen of Egypt's finest Choc Tut's to sweeten any loss you may feel.

J. Pinchart

J. Pinchart
Egyptian Head of Department of Archaeology

PS I hear your ill-fated excavations in search of the lost pharaoh will resume in November, despite your having assured me to the contrary. Let me reiterate my warning. Egyptian artefacts belong to Egypt. Cursed is he who removes them.

Chocolate pharaohs – a sweet gesture or were they filled with something more sinister? Will excavations resume or did Quentin withdraw funding? There is some uncertainty here. Was it a curse or confusion that killed the earl?

While examining the earl's study at Monthaven, I discovered a locked drawer in his desk. Carefully, I pried it open. This is what was inside - why would he keep this locked away?

STOCK REPORT
JANUARY - JULY 1886

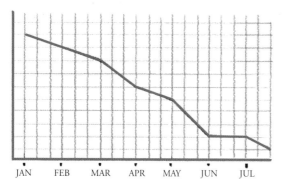

JAN   FEB   MAR   APR   MAY   JUN   JUL

A decline in stock prices. Was the earl relying on this income?

THAM & HOWE

DEWY, CHEATHAM & HOWE
——— SOLICITORS ———

DUE:

Dear Quentin,

Please see attached stock report. ———— £60.00

Income from your father-in-law likely to be severely affected if not severed completely. ———— £49.00

———— £130.00

Please advise,

Donald Dewy

Donald Dewy
Dewy, Cheatham & Howe Solicitors

to be paid
two weeks.

PS Please see attached bill for services.

usiness.

CRISIS SITUATION:
Railways Failing in US

ock prices for the US ilway have continued fall, plunging to the west level in five ars. Stock owners e urged to sell now.

Plagued by delays owing to poor weather and slowed by legislation, the completion of the network has been pushed back by a further three years.

Petunia assured me not to worry and promised she would discuss the matter with her father. I will wait to hear.

5th March

Alas, I can no longer afford to dig in the desert. Who knows what fortunes lie beneath the sand. I have added much of my own for little reward.

Harold must be told that this dig will be the last.

Unpaid bills. Did the earl leave anyone short of money when he died?

EL RASOUL
EXCAVATION SERVICES
CAIRO, EGYPT

Fine for non-payment of invoice dated 14th March, 1886.

£200 – to be paid immediately.

BANK OF
CAIRO

PAY: Quentin Frussup

Seven Hundred Pounds Only £700-

SIGNED: J Pinchart *J. Pinchart*

Selling his artefacts back to Egypt. The earl needed money.

After examining the earl's study, I took the opportunity to pop my head into Lady Monthaven's study. The helpful Ernest had informed me that she would be gone the entire morning, as she was out shopping for supplies for her upcoming trip to Egypt.

21st January

It is my father's money that pays for these excavations – it should be me who gets to go! Q says he likes to dig but refuses to get his hands dirty.

I will write to H and see what he suggests.

Dearest Petunia,

How happy I was to hear that you will be able to fund our next excavation!

I would be happy for you to join our team in Egypt.

I have sent Q a package that should help smooth the way.

H. Caper

Were women permitted to graduate, you would have done so first in your class.
Brava!
Hardman Knox

A skilled Egyptologist? First in her class.

This is to certify that
Petunia Monthaven (née Pearson)
achieved the equivalent of a
1st Class Honours in Egyptology and Hieroglyphics.

Signed ...... *Professor Knox* ....

Saturday, 23rd June

Darling Daughter,

All is sold. Railroads were a
bust. Got out just in time. Let Q
know, or don't. Useless son-in-law
doesn't deserve a penny. I don't
know how you put up with him.

Best go and work out how to spend
it all!

Daddy

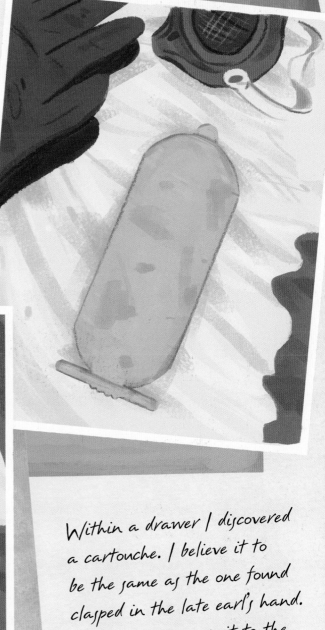

Within a drawer I discovered
a cartouche. I believe it to
be the same as the one found
clasped in the late earl's hand.
Could you compare it to the
earl's sketches and take note
of any differences?

Before leaving, I was able to pick up the family photograph album. I included some of the more interesting pictures here. There was also an intriguing slip of paper tucked inside.

1875 – Engaged

1874 – In love

The Frussups seemed quite the couple in love. Did something turn sour between the pair?

1878 – Our very own treasure!

An unhappy wife –
a threat to his life?

1881 – Caring for new things

1881 – In search of old things

A	B	C	D	E	F	G	H	I	J	K	L	M

N	O	P	Q	R	S	T	U	V	W	X	Y	Z

Below are a few questions to help us dig a little deeper into this accursed crime:

1. A pug's life or a pug's death? What could have killed Anubis?

2. Do you notice anything interesting in Caper's qualifications?

3. Had the earl managed to keep Jacques Pinchart happy?

4. Is there more to Monthaven's finances than has met the eye?

5. How could Lady Monthaven's skill with hieroglyphics help her to avoid the fate of the earl?

An interesting case indeed. What have you deduced from the clues?

Hold the opposite page against a mirror to discover my verdict.

Reader, your painstaking examination of the evidence has been exemplary.

A pharaoh's curse or foul play? Was it bad luck that killed Khara? No, it was treachery and treachery it is again.

A determined archaeologist without funds, a fierce defender of Egyptian antiquities and a wife desperate to dig herself out of obscurity.

Quentin, believing himself bankrupt, had pulled out of future excavations with Harold Caper and had begun to sell off his beloved artefacts to cover unpaid bills. Petunia, tired of her husband's fussy ways and desperate to get back to archaeology, chose not to tell her husband that their money was safe, instead agreeing to give Harold the money under two conditions: that she join the expedition and that Quentin was out of the way.

Caper, determined and skilled, knew just how to do it. He knew how Quentin feared all dust and dirt from having been on digs with him in the past. He had a degree not only in ancient history, but also toxicology, so knew about poisons and applied a toxic dust to the cartouche. He knew the earl would not be able to resist cleaning it off and he also knew it would be the last thing he ever did.

Earl Frussup's fastidiousness proved fatal, as he breathed in the dust and died instantly.

And what of Anubis - the prized pug? Did he fall victim to the same toxic dust? No indeed. Anubis was killed by the curse of an entirely different pharaoh - the Choc Tut's sent by the new Head of Department of Archaeology. Chocolate, though delicious to people, is deadly to dogs.

The Terror of Traymar House

A haunting mystery arrived in the post today. A desperate letter from a Mr Tobias Traymar of Traymar House.

Has some spectre returned from the grave to terrorise the House of Traymar or does this terror have a more earthly origin? I implore you, reader, to lend me your eyes and mind to puzzle through this adventure.

FOR SALE

Traymar House

£2500 ~~£2500~~
~~£1750~~
~~£1000~~
£700

Set in landscaped grounds, this 18-room country house is filled with all the original features you'd expect in a fine rural residence of the period. Includes indoor bathrooms, servants' quarters and gas lighting.

A must-see property

Traymar House
Traymar
Cornwall

15 June

Dear Sherlock,

I am writing to you because I know not where else to turn. The case
I put before you is not criminal (I don't think), but it may cost
me dearly if no explanations are found for the strange goings-on at
Traymar House.

I inherited this estate from my father and though I have done my best
to keep it running, I find myself in the sad situation of having to
sell. The house is too big for me and my elderly aunt, and we have
been unable to make enough money to keep the lights on.

A buyer was lined up and though there were a few questions over
price, the sale was close to being agreed until last week, when a
ghost believed to be long gone returned to haunt us once more. There
has been a sighting in the old nursery and all kinds of odd noises
coming from all over the house with no explanation, as though they
were coming from the walls.

The buyer is spooked and will only commit to buying the property if I
dramatically reduce the asking price.

I am at my wits' end and want to be as far from this place as possible.

Yours desperately,

Tobias Traymar

Tobias Traymar

After the long train ride to Cornwall, I stopped at the Traymar Tavern. As well as refreshment, I found much that was of interest.

Take a look at what I discovered:

TRAYMAR TIMES   11TH JUNE

The Spectre Returns

Reported by Robert Ward

Ghostly goings-on have been reported at Traymar House. Traymar House first earned its place on the ghost map 60 years ago, when the ghost of a young girl who had died many years before was said to haunt the upper floors, often being seen from the windows late at night. But sightings of the ghost stopped suddenly in 1820 and nothing of the ghost has been heard since.

Ghostly sightings, though a boon for the local ghost tour business, couldn't come at a worse time for Tobias Traymar, who has the house on the market. House-hunters love all kinds of inbuilt features, but a ghost is not one of them.

A local man, noticing my interest in the story, struck up a conversation.

WITNESS STATEMENT   Stan Brockles - gardener at Traymar House

Oh! I won't go in the house any more. Not after what I saw. Not that I'm invited in often. Traymar likes the staff to know their place after everything that went on with Dicky. He got mighty jealous of that.

The ghost, or Terror as everyone calls it, was exactly that - terrible. I was putting my tools away in the shed when I saw it. Glowing a monstrous green, a human shape was staring down at me from the third-floor window pointing right at me. No one uses those rooms any more. They used to be the nursery many moons ago. Now, I think they use it for storage. I'll run and get my daughter. She has some stories she can tell you. She was a housemaid at Traymar. Her story will make your blood run cold! We're both glad to be rid of the place.

A terrifying tale indeed, but who is Dicky?

WITNESS STATEMENT   Edmund Markham - tavern owner and ghost tour operator

It's nothing new. The ghost went away for a while but is back with a vengeance. Perhaps angry at Traymar for trying to sell its home from under it. Who knows what a developer would do with the place. They say it's to become a hotel. Hah! Ask to see the guestbook when you're there. I've heard the walls and even the beds are haunted! You couldn't pay me to stay there. If you want to know more about the ghost, take the tour!

Intrigued, I thought I would hear more from the Brockles.

WITNESS STATEMENT   Susan Brockles

I'm glad I left when I did. I was a housemaid at Traymar and never had any trouble until a few months ago, when I began to hear footsteps in the night. It sounded like it was coming from the walls and between the floors. The source of these strange sounds only revealed itself to me once and once was enough, I can assure you. Having been awoken by rushing feet outside my door, I stepped out of my room and saw a tall figure dressed in glowing robes striding down the corridor. I slammed my door, locked it tight and hid under the bed. I handed in my notice at first light. I think it's only Dicky left now. I don't think Dicky would ever leave - no one else will work there.

A ghost who doesn't want the house sold from under it, boosting the local ghost tour trade?

Book signing with local author

Tess Traymar
Tales of Terror

Tess, now in her seventies, resides with her nephew at Traymar House, Cornwall.

Ghost stories are just that – stories. Stories are nothing to be scared of. Ghosts, however? Well, they are something quite different. If a spirit cannot rest easy, neither should you.

Tess Traymar – local celebrity and spooky storyteller. This new terror mustn't be doing her book sales any harm.

My next stop was Traymar House itself, to find out more about these hauntings. I spoke first to Lord Traymar in his study:

WITNESS STATEMENT   Lord Traymar

Thank goodness you have arrived, Mr Holmes. I had chalked these stories up to being just that - stories. I heard the noises at night - again I brushed these off. Old houses make all kinds of noises and this can play tricks on people's imaginations. But it was not a trick of the imagination when I saw the Terror last night at the end of my bed. It appeared, a tall figure, glowing a horrid green, striding towards me. It pointed right at me. I shut my eyes tight and when I opened them, it was gone. I do not know what to do.

Lord Traymar looked as green as the ghost he had described. He stepped out for a moment and while he did so, I took the liberty of looking around.

TRAYMAR HOUSE GUESTBOOK

DATE: 10ᵗʰ June

A strange night indeed. On returning to my room after dinner, I was met with the sight of my bed glowing brightly as if lit by some inner candle. The rumours of the Terror having spooked me, I screamed loudly and ran from the room.

I met the butler, Richard, in the hallway, who hurried me downstairs to collect myself with a hot cocoa. He left me in the library, saying he would investigate further. Richard returned some 20 minutes or so later. He had investigated my room thoroughly and found nothing untoward. I accompanied him back and, indeed, the room looked warm and inviting. There was something different about the bed, but when he extinguished the lights it was clear it did not glow. I cannot say what took place - perhaps my eyes played tricks on me or perhaps I was exhausted from my journey. But I will say I was more exhausted the next day, as I hardly got a wink of sleep. I said my goodbyes very early the next day.

BIJOUX
ESTATE AGENT

Dear Lord Traymar,

I am afraid the interested party has withdrawn their offer on the estate. The stories of the 'ghost' are all over the village. They are scaring away buyers before they even visit, making it a poor candidate for a hotel. Hotels need guests, after all.

I assure you we are doing everything we can to market your estate, but there is very little interest in homes with built-in horrors.

We do have one interested party, but the price (even after your many reductions) is still too high.

Would you consider coming down to £500? I realise this is well below what a house like Traymar should command but, alas, an estate is only worth what someone is willing to pay.

Yours regretfully,

Monty Bijoux

Monty Bijoux
Estate Agent

Last Will and Testament

Terrence Traymar

I leave the house and the estate to my son, Tobias Traymar, in the hope that he will keep it as a home for my dear sister, Theresa (Tess).

And to Richard, the son of my late butler Edmund (Eddie) Simms, I leave the sum of £500 and the assurance that while a Traymar lives at Traymar, he will have a home.

Signed: *T. Traymar*

Dearest Toby,

I find myself unwell and no longer able to walk. I must return home to Traymar. It has been so long since I lived there. I wonder if it has changed much.

Please could you arrange someone to meet my train.

Yours truly,

Tess

Did Tess bring anything home with her?

Aunt Tess's return coincides with the return of the Terror of Traymar. I took a moment to explore her ground-floor suite.

Darling & Co BOOKS

Dear Miss Traymar,

So glad your research is well under way for the long-awaited follow-up to your 1835 bestseller – *Tales of Terror*.

We've had many requests for this since the renewed haunting, so get writing!

I wondered if this phosphorous research might help at all in your plotting.

Yours sincerely,

J Darling

J. Darling

Phosphorous
Discovered in 1669 by Hennig Brand

Brand called his discovery 'cool fire' because of its glow-in-the-dark properties. Phosphorous is commonly used in garden fertilisers.

Red phosphorous, shown here in powder form

Boosting sales. Is Tess plotting more than just her next book?

What does she plan to buy with the proceeds?

11th June

It's so wonderful to be back at Traymar. So many fond memories of the mischief I used to get up to with Terrence. It would appear some of that mischief still haunts our old nursery. If only I wasn't confined to this wheelchair, so I could go up and investigate myself. I shall content myself with my writing. Who knows, if I earn enough, I could buy the house from Tobias and ease his money worries once and for all. I would be so sad to leave this place.

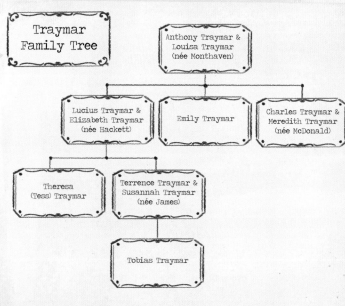

An interesting family tree. Tobias is the last Traymar.

While in Tess's suite I had a glance through her collection of family photographs and sketches. Do you notice anything interesting about them?

The girls and me in our first year at St Kate's School for Young Ladies. 1820

Terrence

Toby

Dicky

Sometimes friends can become closer than family, it seems.

I needed to know more about the house and this ghost. I went to the house's library, which was very dusty. This Simms must be overworked.

I found these plans. Can you see anything of interest?

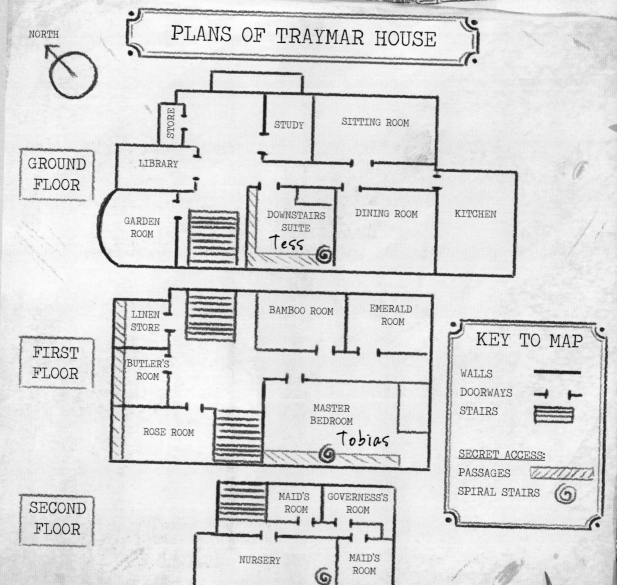

PLANS OF TRAYMAR HOUSE

NORTH

GROUND FLOOR

STORE

LIBRARY

STUDY

SITTING ROOM

GARDEN ROOM

DOWNSTAIRS SUITE
Tess

DINING ROOM

KITCHEN

FIRST FLOOR

LINEN STORE

BUTLER'S ROOM

ROSE ROOM

BAMBOO ROOM

EMERALD ROOM

MASTER BEDROOM
Tobias

SECOND FLOOR

MAID'S ROOM

GOVERNESS'S ROOM

NURSERY

MAID'S ROOM

KEY TO MAP

WALLS
DOORWAYS
STAIRS

SECRET ACCESS:
PASSAGES
SPIRAL STAIRS

One book was off the shelf and not dusty –

Tales of Terror by Tess Traymar

A particular passage caught my eye and I made a note of it here:

'The glowing ghost stood pointing through the window...
pointing at what the faint-hearted maiden would never know,
for she fainted clear away. When she awoke, it was gone.'

The appearance of this ghost sounds very familiar.

TRAYMAR TIMES

YOUR LOCAL NEWSPAPER   MARCH, 1820

Traymar's ghost: fact or fiction?

Reported by Amelia Drage

Troublesome goings-on at Traymar House. Tales of ghosts, bumps in the night and glowing spectres.

"We have lost six staff in the last month alone, including a tutor and two governesses. Our children will have to be sent away to school. The only member of staff who has remained with us over the years is Simms, who is clearly made of sterner stuff than most." commented Lady Traymar.

We also spoke to Abigale Jones, who worked as a scullery maid at Traymar House. "I'd heard about the hauntings before I took the job but didn't think much about it. My

bedroom was next to the nursery and I often heard ghostly wailings in the night. I even saw a figure gliding along the corridors. I wish I'd listened to the warnings!"

Richard Simms has been at the house as long as the current Lord Traymar himself and must know every inch of it. I put my head around his door to see if I could discover any trace of this terror.

3rd July

An interesting letter?

Dearest Dicky,

What a comfort you have been to me in my old age. Tobias being away I don't know how I would have managed the house without you or your grandfather and father before you.

You have been like a son to me and I know as long as you are at Traymar the house will be safe.

I leave you my watch, so that you remember our time together!Ha ha!

Take care of my son. He is not like us and has much to learn from you.

Yours sincerely,

T. Traymar

Terrence Traymar

Jobs to do today:

~~Polish silver~~
~~Dust library~~
Pay invoices
Visit bank
Tend to garden

It seems there was quite the bond between the former Lord Traymar and 'Dicky'.

BIJOUX
ESTATE AGENT

Dear Mr Simms,

Thank you for your interest in Traymar House. I am afraid the owner is unwilling to sell the home for such a low sum at this time.

Just between you and me, if the hauntings were to continue, I think you may be able to call Traymar home sooner rather than later. We shall see.

Yours sincerely,

Monty Bijoux

Monty Bijoux
Estate Agent

FOR SALE

MEMO
From: Tobias Traymar
To: Richard Simms

Dicky! Dear boy, I have had to let the gardener go. Do you think you might be able to have a tinker about out there? Don't want it turning into a jungle and putting off buyers. Here's a key to Stan's shed. Should find everything you need in there.

I bought you this gardening book!

Oh! and remember, we have guests tonight. Please make sure the Rose Room has fresh linen.

Your friend,

Tobias

CHAPTER 7
Understanding Phospherous-based fertilisers

will grow much faster and mature earlier than a plant that has not been grown with phosphorus. Without phosphorus, plants can exhibit a purple hue owing to the photosynthetic process being affected. Plants may also wilt, become stunted and lack fruit or flowers.

67

Wednesday, 4th June

A hotel! Strangers sleeping at Traymar! Dear Terrence would hate the very idea. It must be stopped. People must be discouraged from staying here. I shall make sure they get no rest. Tess's return has given me wonderful ideas. Dear lady. Far from making trouble for her, my meddling could lead to a new life for her. How Terrence would have loved that.

I wish Tobias would stop calling me Dicky. That is what his dear father called me and what I am known as to my friends. Tobias is not my friend. To him, I am, and always will be, Richard.

A strained relationship between these childhood companions?

Below are a few questions to shed some
light on these ghostly goings-on:

1. Do the ghost sightings have anything in common?

2. Who might be willing or able to pay a reduced price for Traymar?

3. Who has access to the secret passageways at Traymar House?

4. Why might the hauntings have halted in 1820?

5. Can you dig up anything of interest in the garden shed?

Perhaps the case is not
quite as chilling as it
may seem.

Hold the opposite page
to a mirror to discover
my verdict.

Well done, reader for coming to a natural, rather than supernatural, conclusion to this most haunting of cases... the butler did it.

The overworked Richard (Dicky) Simms, loyal to the household for so long, was desperate that Traymar House should not be sold outside of the family. Though not a blood relative, Simms had lived at the house since he was born and his father had also worked there serving the then Lord of Traymar. Lord Traymar took a shine to the young boy, who was similar in age to his own son but more similar in temperament to himself. Lord Terrence had left Simms some money in his will, but it was not enough to buy the house unless he brought the price down as far as he could. The return of Tess Traymar and her stories gave him just what he needed: a plan that could work.

It was a clever plan, but even clever people make mistakes. Simms, having soaked sheets in glow-in-the-dark phosphorous so he could pose as a ghost, accidentally mixed them up with the sheets for the Rose Room. A fact that only became apparent after dark.

And what of the original terror? Why, this was Tess and her brother, Terrence, terrorising their tutors and governesses until they had to be sent away to school. Tess was so inspired she took to writing ghost stories and had them published. Tess, no matter how much she may not want the house to be sold and despite the fact that the return of the ghost is boosting sales, could not be responsible for the Terror's return, as she is now confined to a wheelchair.

The Adventure of the Vanishing Lord

A most curious case of magic and mystery that I am sure will reveal itself to be even more extraordinary than it at first appears.
Can you solve the case and find the missing magician?

VANISHING MAGICIAN FAILS TO REAPPEAR

Lord Fitzgibbon before his disappearance

An audience was left stunned at Lord Fitzgibbon's show, 'Magical Secrets Revealed', when the vanishing lord failed to reappear following his final trick. Lord Marmeduke Fitzgibbon, who performs under the name 'The Fantastic Fitz', had hired the Mandrake Theatre to display his mania for all things magical to a select group of family and friends, as well as fellow members from the Society of Magicians. His whereabouts is yet to be confirmed.

A statement from the raven-haired chief wizard from the Society, the Great Suprendo, said, "It is clear from his disappearance that Lord Fitzgibbon is a far superior sorcerer than any of us had suspected."

Witnesses with information are asked to contact Mr S. Holmes.

We were in the middle of performing our final illusion.

Marmie (that's my little pet name for Marmeduke) stepped to
the front, as if to take his final bow, when a silk curtain
cascaded from the gods, leaving only his shadow in view.
This all went to plan. The curtain fell and I walked up
to it with a lighted taper. I lit the corner of the curtain,
which burned to nothing, to reveal that Marmie had
disappeared. It is rather a lovely trick when it works. Well,
I guess it did work, perhaps a little too well.

I ran to the back of the stage to open the magic cabinet
for Marmie to step out, but he wasn't there. He wasn't
anywhere. In his place, pinned to the false back of the
cabinet by a dagger, were these two playing cards. What can
it mean?

I can't think what went wrong. Please, Mr Holmes. Please
help me find my Marmie. I cannot live thinking that I have
somehow magicked him away. He was such a gentle soul,
loved by everyone who knew him.

*Even the gentlest of lords have
enemies who would do them harm...*

*Turn the page to begin
the search for this most
mysterious magician.*

A compelling case indeed. Let us examine Lord Marmeduke's dressing room at the Mandrake Theatre. I do not believe anything to have been disturbed since the disappearance. It would appear he had a few cards up his sleeve. What can you deduce from this curious scene?

HYPNOSIS IN A HURRY

This cert__fies that Lord Ma___rmeduke is a memb___er of the BROTHERHOOD ___OF MAGICIANS

PLAYING ·CARDS·

Meet the Midgicians!

The most magical family in Londo

I found this interesting code upon the desk. What could it mean?
Does the cipher key give us any clues to Lord Marmeduke's location?

	A	B	C	D	E	F	G	H	I	J	K	L	M
A♣	A	2	3	4	5	6	7	8	9	10	J	Q	K

	N	O	P	Q	R	S	T	U	V	W	X	Y	Z
A♠	A	2	3	4	5	6	7	8	9	10	J	Q	K

A page torn from Marmeduke's journal:

<u>Wednesday, 6th October, 1886</u>
Dues paid. The Great S visited me at home.
A real honour.

<u>Friday, 8th October, 1886</u>
Midday. Lunch with the Great Stupendo.

Meeting did not go well. Society claimed the chief wizard, the Great Suprendo, had never heard of me. They had no record of my having paid my dues and would therefore not be able to grant me my promotion to sorcerer. I have been wronged and tomorrow night, I will reveal all of their secrets.

<u>Saturday, 9th October, 1886</u>
This will be my final show as the Fantastic Fitz. The Society will never see me as a magician again.

Must remember to ask Marianne to invite the Lannisters over for bridge next Sunday.

Stupendo or Suprendo?

Is Lord Marmeduke a careless speller or are these two different people?

Lord Marmeduke was last seen on stage. It is assumed he escaped by the trapdoor as planned. But where did he go from there? Perhaps these plans from the theatre manager's office can shed some light on the magician's mysterious next steps:

MANDRAKE THEATRE
MANAGER'S UNDERGROUND PLAN
---- PRIVATE ----

MAGICAL CABINET

STAGE

DRESSING ROOM 1

STORAGE ROOM

TO G7

DRESSING ROOM 2

TO TRICKSTER'S TROVE

COSTUME STORE

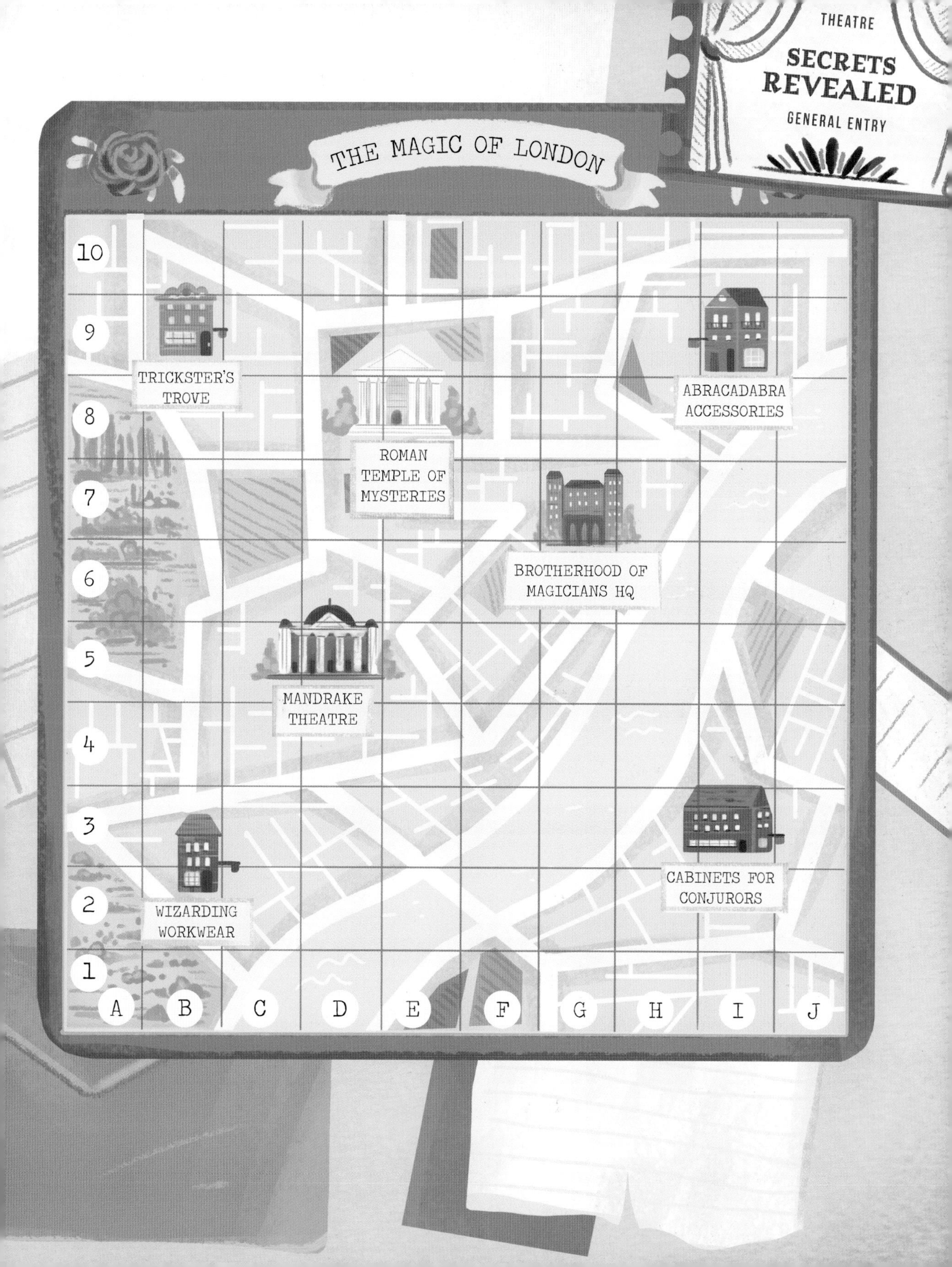

THEATRE
SECRETS REVEALED
GENERAL ENTRY
THE MAGIC OF LONDON
TRICKSTER'S TROVE
ROMAN TEMPLE OF MYSTERIES
ABRACADABRA ACCESSORIES
BROTHERHOOD OF MAGICIANS HQ
MANDRAKE THEATRE
WIZARDING WORKWEAR
CABINETS FOR CONJURORS
10
9
8
7
6
5
4
3
2
1
A
B
C
D
E
F
G
H
I
J

The trail leads to the HQ of the Brotherhood. Could they hold among their secrets the whereabouts of Lord Marmeduke? Here is some of the evidence I collected on my visit:

BROTHERHOOD OF MAGICIANS

Congratulations on becoming a magical member of the Brotherhood of Magicians.

Progress through the ranks of our esteemed Brotherhood is determined by a magician's magical merit and financial commitment.

Entry – Apprentice

Level One – Warlock

Level Two – Magician

Level Three – Sorcerer

Level Four – Grand Wizard

Cheques for advancement to be made payable to Landon Midge – the Great Suprendo.

The Great Suprendo and Council of Grand Wizards wish you luck on your magical journey!

Membership entitles you to 10% off at magical merchants across London:

- Abracadabra Accessories
- Cabinets for Conjurors
- Dillon's Doves (bunnies also)
- Entrance to the Roman Temple of Mysteries
- ~~Trickster's Trove~~
- Wizarding Workwear

<u>Conditions of membership</u>
The Brotherhood is a family and all families have secrets. These secrets must be kept. Failure to do so by a member will have dire consequences both within the Brotherhood and without.

Welcome to the Brotherhood – the Great Suprendo!

Did the Brotherhood fear for the safety of their secrets in the hands of Lord Marmeduke?

WITNESS STATEMENT

Mildred Clay
- receptionist

The Great Suprendo is abroad until Saturday. Please take a look at his appointment book and let me know if there is a time which he is available that would work for you.

MONDAY	10 a.m.	Hypnosis 301 - The Art of Forgetting
TUESDAY	10 a.m. Noon	Sleight of Hand 101 Lunch with L.M.
WEDNESDAY	10 a.m. 1 p.m.	Badminton Take doves to vet
THURSDAY	10 a.m.	Dentist
FRIDAY	12 p.m. 6 p.m.	Lunch with Fantastic Fitz? ~~Dinner with L.M.~~
SATURDAY	9 a.m. 9 p.m.	Breakfast M.F. The Art of Forgetting practical exam.
SUNDAY		

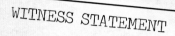

I liberated last week's page for investigation.

Could Lord Marmeduke really have disappeared into the magical ether never to return? What is there to this meeting that took place on the Wednesday before his disappearance? Perhaps a visit to the lord's study will shed some light on these shadowy goings-on...

WITNESS STATEMENT
Thomas Goddard - butler

A funny fellow. Jet-black hair. Left a terrible black stain on the headrest of his lordship's second-best chair. I've tried everything to remove it. His lordship seemed most pleased when he departed. He brought all manner of funny devices with him. Wealthy lords have time for some odd hobbies.

BROTHERHOOD OF MAGICIANS

Your work as a magician has been noticed.

You will hear from G.S. in good time. Once your payment has been received, you will become a sorcerer among friends.

Signed,

L. Midge

The Fantastic Fitz

TONIGHT ONLY!
AT THE MANDRAKE THEATRE

ACCEPT THIS GIFT COURTESY OF
TRICKSTER'S TROVE

To a fine sorcerer!

L. <u>Midge</u>

L. MIDGE
THE GREAT
STUPENDO

 **Bank of the CITY**

PAY: L. Midge

Twenty Pounds Only
£20-

GREAT STUPENDO STORE TO CLOSE

Reported by R.G. Watts

The magical superstore Trickster's Trove, run by the Great Stupendo, is set to close later this month. Falling profits and high rent in this Central London location has forced the hand of proprietor Leonard Midge. Aspiring magicians will now have to travel to newly opened Magical Moments in Soho for supplies of magical accessories and ... perhaps ...

Business has gone bad. Has the businessman gone bad also?

I felt compelled by a mysterious force to visit *Trickster's Trove* to discover what secrets might be hiding there. Here is what I was able to discover:

I took a look in the back office. A mess it was indeed. I suspect a disturbance.

A mysterious trapdoor! Where might it lead?

BROTHERHOOD OF MAGICIANS

Dearest Leonard,

Your business membership with the Brotherhood is revoked for non-payment of dues.

I know you are family, but at the Brotherhood we are all a family and need to pitch in.

Yours regretfully,

L. Midge

Family members need to pitch in. What else did they need to do?

BROTHERHOOD OF MAGICIANS

Application for Grand Wizard Council for L. Midge:
DENIED

RAVEN'S WING

Dye it black —
don't look back.

034

The world of magic is an illusion. Now, it is rich lords with money who advance up the craft hierarchy. Skilled magicians are cast out for lack of funds. Well, I have taken my share from the lord. Ha ha.

L was very angry. I think he is jealous of my literary future. He said the Brotherhood would not allow my book to publish. There will be no book because I will have no memories of magic. How could I <u>ever forget?</u> I am a greater magician than he will ever be. What can he do? He would never hurt me.

I intend to spend some time abroad, so I may complete the book in peace.

Interesting. How could he ever forget? Is there an art of forgetting?

WHITE SHIP COMPANY

PASSAGE TO: .... Barcelona
DAY OF TRAVEL: .... Sunday
PAYMENT: £60

PEREGRINE BOOKS

Dear Leonard,

I'm delighted to inform you that we enjoyed the first chapter and would like to publish your book entitled:

How it's Done - Magical Secrets Revealed
by L. Midge.

Please accept this advance of £40.

Yours sincerely,

Hector Lowe

A book no Brother would want to see the light of day.

Here are a few questions to help focus the mind on the evidence at hand:

1. Is there a difference between Stupendo and Suprendo?

2. What do you make of the books in Lord Marmeduke's dressing room?

3. Does anywhere on *The Magic of London* map sound familiar?

4. The Great Suprendo is a busy man. What do you make of his schedule?

5. How could Leonard Midge ever forget?

Have you arrived at a suitable conclusion?

Hold the opposite page against a mirror to reveal the true fate of Lord Marmeduke.

Reader - the clues have led to a sad truth. The Great Supremo and Stupendo (Landon and Leonard) are brothers in the real as well as magical sense. Torn apart by ambition and pride, they both moved in the same magical circle, but Leonard became frustrated and jealous of te success of his brother. He decided to cut all ties in a most dramatic way. Leonard was in the process of writing a book revealing all the magical secrets of the Brotherhood - a book he planned to finish writing in Barcelona.

Leonard's plan was similar to that of our vanished Lord Marmeduke. Lord Marmeduke had planned to reveal the secrets of the Brotherhood during his performance at the Mandrake Theatre. He was angry when they claimed to have no knowledge of his payment to become a sorcerer. This was because he had actually paid the money to Leonard (who was in need of money for his passage to Barcelona), who had posed as Landon by dyeing his hair.

This proved unnecessary. On the morning before the performance, Landon revealed a plan over breakfast for Marmeduke to demonstrate his magical skill, prove his loyalty to the Brotherhood and put an end to Leonard's treachery. Marmeduke was to disappear at the end of his show through the tunnel beneath the theatre and meet with Landon and Leonard (who had been kidnapped by Landon) at the Brotherhood HQ.

There, Leonard was to be hypnotised to erase all of his magical knowledge and thoughts of treachery. Marmeduke then made sure Leonard made it to Barcelona before returning and rejoining the Brotherhood as a sorcerer.

Dear Reader,

Congratulations!

Thanks to your efforts and powers of deduction, these most sinister cases have been solved and the fate of the villains responsible now rests in the hands of the courts.

You have expertly unravelled the mystery of the stolen ruby, baked into a most delicious cherry cake. You have helped to bring a poisoner to justice and allowed the butler of Monthaven Manor some closure on his master's premature departure. You uncovered the true identity of the ghost haunting Traymar House and you even aided in making a magician reappear.

It is of great assurance for me to know, should I have need, a fellow mind capable of solving the seemingly unsolvable is available to assist in bringing comfort to the poor souls who seek it at my door.

I can only hope, once word reaches the press, villains intent on committing heinous acts against others take heed and reconsider. However, if my experience as the world's most famous detective has taught me anything, it is that while there exists a cloak of darkness there will be those intent on concealing their true nature amongst its inky folds.

Until next time, reader.

Yours faithfully,

Sherlock Holmes